Learning to Fly

Paul Yee

Orca soundings

Orca Book Publishers

Library and Archives Canada Cataloguing in Publication

Yee, Paul

Learning to fly / written by Paul Yee.

(Orca soundings)
ISBN 978-1-55143-955-6 (bound).--ISBN 978-1-55143-953-2 (pbk.)

I. Title. II. Series.
PS8597.E3L42 2008   jC813'.54   C2008-903026-5

Summary: Jason, a recent immigrant from China,
makes some bad decisions as he comes to terms
with small-town racism while trying to fit in.

First published in the United States, 2008
Library of Congress Control Number: 2008928578

Orca Book Publishers gratefully acknowledges the support for its publishing
programs provided by the following agencies: the Government of Canada
through the Book Publishing Industry Development Program and the Canada
Council for the Arts, and the Province of British Columbia through the BC
Arts Council and the Book Publishing Tax Credit.

Cover design by Teresa Bubela
Cover photography by Getty Images

ORCA BOOK PUBLISHERS
PO Box 5626, STN. B
VICTORIA, BC CANADA
V8R 6S4

ORCA BOOK PUBLISHERS
PO Box 468
CUSTER, WA USA
98240-0468

www.orcabook.com
Printed and bound in Canada.
Printed on 100% PCW recycled paper.

11 10 09 08 • 4 3 2 1

For Jenny Khaki,
whose cooking keeps me going.

Chapter One

Three more hours. One hundred and eighty minutes.

Milson Mall is busy on weekends, so I am forced to help at my mom's deli.

Ten thousand, eight hundred seconds. Ten million, eight hundred thousand milli-seconds. Then the mall closes, and I can go roll a joint and inhale those sweet, sweet fumes. Then all the crap in my life will float away, just like the smoke.

From below, a little girl hands me two dollars. Is she mumbling or am I stupid? I lean over the counter and ask, politely as usual, "What can I get you?"

This time I think I hear "cookies."

"What kind?" Now my words are loud, and strained if you listen hard.

She looks away and strands of yellow hair swirl up.

"What kind?" I ask again, wanting to reach out and twist her ear hard.

After we exchange oatmeal cookies and cash, she runs off. Her mother, a plump woman guarding a stroller, stands far back. It is as if she's worried that just standing close to the baking will make her fatter.

The next person has a belly that pokes out like a prize-winning pumpkin. He orders coffee and apple pie.

"What do you take?" I ask.

"Huh?" He frowns.

"How do you take your coffee?" I speak louder. "Black? Cream? Sugar?"

"Oh! Just milk."

My English is not bad, but people do not hear me. They see a Chinese face, and right away they think my English will be poor and broken.

Bland music fills the mall. Bland shoppers stroll through, licking ice-cream cones. The air in here is stale. This whole town is stale.

Four kids from school enter through the main door. Right away I squat and pretend to straighten the trays of squares and tarts in the display case. I pray that none of the kids will come near the deli. Through the glass I see one I think of as "sweat-shirt girl" because she is always wearing the same shirt. She is looking over here, searching for a target. Usually she nudges and calls to her friends, and then they all stare at me, giggling or laughing. I don't even know their names.

"*Jie-xin*, where are you?"

I stand up as Aunt Mei hurries in with Josh. She watches my little brother on weekends.

"I need to pee-pee," he says.

"You take him," I say, turning away. Aunt Mei and I speak Chinese.

"You take him!" she retorts. "In the washroom, women do not like to see little boys running around."

"I'm too busy."

"You have no one here!"

Ma calls from the back, "Jason, take him!"

I edge away from her voice.

"Right now!" Ma shouts.

I swear under my breath and rip off my apron. Josh smiles at me. I march him past the shoe shop, the drugstore and the crafts place. I press him so close to the walls that he squeals in protest. Maybe we can get through the food court without the kids seeing us. Why are the washrooms right by the eating tables?

I slow down to keep pace with strolling shoppers so that we will not be noticed. My eyes stay down and watch the ugly brown tiles rush by. Then I hear the guys' voices.

"Hey, Jason-baby!"

"Daddy!"

"I need to go pooh-pooh too, Papa! Can you take me?"

We rush into the washroom and into a stall. I slam the door and stand Josh on the rim of the bowl. Someone did not flush the toilet. Spongy brown coils float below. Ugh!

"Hurry!" I growl.

His eyes are big. "Were those people laughing at you?" he asks.

"Who?"

"Those people."

"Don't know them. Come on, hurry!"

Josh is only three. He is fourteen years younger than me. No one in my class has a brother or sister who is so many years behind. Everyone pretends to think I am Josh's father because it is so funny, and because my dad is not living with us. When I arrived in this town, Celine Lapointe, the girl who was assigned as my "buddy," told me that a thirteen-year-old in grade eight got pregnant. I acted as if it was no big deal.

When we come out, the kids are waiting. They sit close to the entrance. I can see their faces clearly, all pale and white. They jeer at me.

"Daddy, bring the kid to school."

"Show us how you change diapers and wipe ass!"

"Hey, are you breast-feeding, Daddy?"

I check my watch. Time is crawling. Back at the deli, Ma asks brightly, "Did you see your friends?"

Friends? What friends? I make a grunting sound.

"At school you must make friends," Ma adds. With no customers at the deli counter, she speaks Chinese too. "Bring them home and welcome them."

I would sooner slit my wrists, I think.

"Your English will improve with new friends."

Shut up, I want to shout. You know nothing! You think it's easy to make friends?

To have friends you must be cool. You must wear the right clothes. You must know how to make people laugh. And you must look like everyone else.

Ma lied to me. Before moving here, she told me that many Chinese people lived in North America. She did not say they all lived in the big cities. In Milson, we are the only Chinese. I can never trust Ma again.

Chapter Two

"Stop!" barks a voice. "Police!"

Two people dash through the mall. They run so fast that they blur. They crash through the crowds, chased by the dark blue and shiny black of two cops. People hop out of the way and flatten themselves against the walls. At the water fountain, the two suspects break off from each other and sprint toward the far ends of the mall.

Aunt Mei scoops Josh up and runs to the back of the deli. Ma yanks open the cash drawer and whips the tray to safety.

Shoppers hurry toward the exit doors, but I hear no fire alarm. In fact, a deathly silence hangs over the place. We have been told by mall security that a steady clang means that store owners should leave the building quickly. A stop-and-start clang means we should hide inside our stores for safety. Or is it a steady clang that tells us to stay? I can't recall.

Ma orders me to stay, but I rush after the chase. Did the cops pull out their guns? Hey, if they shoot someone, they'll shut down the mall with long loops of yellow warning tape. That would be great news. At last I would get part of a Saturday to myself.

One cop has thrown someone to the ground and is cuffing his hands behind his back. The man is kicking and growling. He has long black hair and wears faded jeans and a jean jacket. A bunch of crests are sewn onto the back. I've seen them before. When the cop pulls him to his feet, I realize it is Chief. He goes to my school. His real name is Charles, but he got his nickname because he is First Nations.

"Leaders of Indian bands are called chiefs," Celine told me.

It made sense then. "Indian" was the word we had used in China. There, the word had three parts: *yin-di-an*.

Celine said that the people who lived here first recently chose the name "First Nations." They had been called "Indians" by Columbus. That was a mistake. The explorer thought he was in India after crossing the Pacific Ocean in 1492. I didn't know any of this until Celine explained it to me.

When school started this fall, Celine Lapointe walked me through the building and pointed out the washrooms. She helped me with English homework. She introduced the teachers and warned her friends to treat me nicely. But no one bothered to come near me. She also explained the rules. We grade elevens could talk with any grade twelve student who might be in one of our split classes, but we could never look at anyone from a lower grade. Celine was one of the top students in my grade, and very popular.

I should have tried harder to be her friend. But I never fit in with her crowd. They spoke too fast. They laughed at things I didn't understand. When Celine tried to explain their jokes, I felt even more stupid. I started staying away from them. That meant I saw Celine less and less.

Chief grins at the cop. His teeth are bright against his dark skin. He is tall and solidly built.

"Hey, why don't you leave him alone?" A First Nations shopper glares at the cop, her arms crossed over her chest. She's small but not one bit afraid. "He's just a kid. What's he done?"

"Why don't you shut up?" someone shouts from the crowd.

The cop does not say a word.

"You cops always pick on us." The woman scowls at the circle of people around her. "It's not fair."

I draw back at the sight of the kids from the food court. They are across from me, holding soft drinks and sucking on plastic straws. Their eyes are cool and uncaring. At school, they don't mix with the First Nations kids.

Chief catches my eye, but I look away. Who needs trouble with the cops? Celine told me Chief had been captain of the school football team until he hooked up with the potheads. In the hallway, she also pointed out his sister Diane, who is only in grade ten but is already president of the First Nations Club.

The other cop comes up. She's pushing someone who also has his hands cuffed. As soon as I see his face, I leave. It's The Man. He's my dealer. I buy my pot from him.

The shoppers are clapping. This town loves law and order. The newspaper is always printing stories about break-and-enters, stolen cars or headstones over-turned at the graveyard. The editor blames young people first. Then he blames parents who do not keep track of where their teenage children are. That would be my mother.

"The more they arrest, the better it is," mutters Aunt Mei. A sour smile twists her face as she watches the cops march their prisoners through the mall and out the door. "I should never have left that coin purse in the car," she adds. "I bought it at the Huashan temple in Shanghai."

One month after we moved to Milson, someone smashed the back window of Ma's car. Inside, the only thing of value was the little bag of coins for the parking meters. It held less than ten bucks. When we reported it, the police shrugged.

"It cost me four hundred dollars to fix that window." Ma sighs. "That was worse."

"In China, things were never this bad," sniffs her sister.

"Then let's go home," I say. "Let's go back to China right away."

It's what I want most of all in this world. I know we would all be happier there. I would become the perfect son. I promised Ma that. I would do any chore and every job she threw at me. Empty the trash, mop the bathroom, play fewer video games. But Ma ignores me. She has heard it before.

I lean over the Chinese newspaper. It is only two weeks late. Ma won't let me read it when I'm working. She fears it may insult customers, but right now she's busy talking to Aunt Mei.

"At least in China people respect the law," she says, thrusting the money tray back into the cash register. "Here lawyers have more power than the police. Robbers have more rights than their victims."

"And those Native people are the worst!" exclaims Aunt Mei. "Newspapers say the courts and judges are gentler when it is time to punish them. It's the law of the land! It's madness!"

Aunt Mei is waltzing through this life while her eyes are taped shut. She believes she is happy because she lives in North America. Many people in China want to move here, but it's not easy to get in. Aunt Mei acts as if she is smarter and better than the local people. She loves to brag about China: factories sprout up on farmland, the number of rich people is growing and shoppers can buy foreign goods. Sounds funny, doesn't it? She's here, but she thinks things are better back in China. That's how some immigrants are. They come here hoping for a better life but don't find it. So, to make themselves feel better, they praise life in China and think that one day they may go back. Me, I want to go back to China because I fit in there, not because it's better.

So why the hell is Aunt Mei living here?

I know why. So she can push Ma to complain about rising taxes, the high prices for food and the icy winters. So they can grumble about their neighbors, about how those people's mouths smile and spout nice words while their eyes stay cold and hard.

The two women never mention what really makes Ma sad. My dad, Ba, left her for another woman. He dumped Ma, even after she traveled across the Pacific Ocean and bore him another son. What a jerk Ba turned out to be. He had gone ahead of us to North America to find work and set up house here. Nobody ever thought he would get a new girlfriend too.

Ma and I arrived two years after him. My brother was born a year later. Then, right after Josh's first birthday, Ba moved out. Ma cried for hours and wouldn't step outside the house for weeks. When I finished grade ten earlier this year, we moved to Milson. I didn't want to come here. All my friends lived in the city. But Ma said she needed to get far away from Ba, so she grabbed the chance to buy the deli.

I hate my father a million times more than my mother does. If my parents were still married, I could head back to China right away, by myself. But as long as Ma lives alone here, I have to stay and look after her.

"You stay away from those Native people," Aunt Mei says to me. "They will lead you into trouble."

She knows nothing. Nothing!

Chapter Three

Today is a bad day. Very bad.

First class of the day, I get dragged to the front of the room. Lines of numbers and letters run across the blackboard like little frightened birds. I feel people staring.

"Show the class how to prove this identity," sings out the math teacher as she hands me some chalk. "It's easy."

What is she talking about?

"I just gave you the model," she adds. "Do you need a hint to get started?"

In English, the teacher springs a surprise quiz on the class. Everyone groans. I did not read the novel, so my sheet is blank.

Mr. Mills waves it around and exclaims, "Look, Mr. Shen doesn't waste ink or paper! We should call him Mr. Green!"

You idiot! I shout in my head.

In chemistry, no one wants to be my lab partner, so I do the lab alone. The others in class finish ahead of me and find free time to visit and chat. Nobody comes near me in the back row. I have to read the lesson, tinker with the pipettes, read the lesson again, pour the solvents into small flasks, reread the lesson, measure the changes and write down the results. If only I had four pairs of hands. What if I record false numbers and see if the teacher can spot them?

At lunchtime, I run across the football field to the oak trees. It's where the potheads usually hang out. No one is there today. I debate whether or not to smoke a joint if I'm there by myself. In the end I do.

I light up and hold the smoke as long as my lungs can bear. When I exhale, the smoke takes away the pain. It's as if a clanking, belching garbage truck ran over my chest earlier. Now the ground beneath me softens and the breeze cools my anger and carries it away. The green grass and blue sky leave me feeling calm and rested.

"Mr. Shen."

The name hammers at me. Hey, it's mine!

"Mr. Shen, wake up!"

I sit bolt upright.

"Mr. Shen, didn't you go to bed last night?"

"What? And make more babies?" someone whispers.

My classmates snicker. They think potheads live on a cloud. I think smoking pot makes me more alert. At least when I'm awake.

I look straight ahead. Mr. Cooper is the social studies teacher. From behind his thick beard, he usually mumbles and yells in slang. He thinks those words help him to *connect* with students. I can't always follow his meanings. He wears bright Hawaiian shirts and tons of fake gold around his neck and fingers. No teacher in China ever dressed like him. He has no idea how stupid he looks.

"Do you know where you are, Mr. Shen?" he asks.

His voice is sharp. His questions are meant to cut and claw into me. I force myself to nod.

"Where are you, then? Tell the class, so we can be sure that you are really with us."

The smoke has relaxed me too much. I giggle.

"What's so funny, Mr. Shen?"

I shake my head and clench my teeth to stop the chuckles. I can't. From the corner of my eye, I see someone rolling her gaze to the ceiling.

"What class are you in?"

"Socials. Socials eleven." I can barely heave out the words. The giggling controls me one hundred percent. I drop my head to hide my face and stare at the floor.

"Which country are we looking at today?"

I gasp and spray out the answer. "China!"

"And what are we looking at in China?"

"Human rights, sir!"

My whole body jangles from the crazy giggling.

"Then tell us something about life in that police state."

Those words sober me. After a while, when I do not answer, Cooper glances at Celine. She must have told him what I mentioned to her about China. What a big mouth she has.

"Did you ever see a Chinese police officer arrest someone?" he demands.

I shake my head.

"Are you sure?"

I nod.

"You never saw the police arrest workers outside a law office? Injured workers who were using crutches?"

One day, when Celine told me her mother worked as a lawyer, I described what I had seen outside a Chinese law office. By the time the police hauled away the lawyer's clients, blood was smeared over the walls and sidewalk. The crutches were snapped into small pieces. When I went back the next day, I could still see the dark stains on the stone.

Mr. Cooper tilts his head and gives me an icy look. He speaks slowly, as if I am a half-wit. "Let's get our facts straight. You moved here from China, didn't you?"

I nod.

"Why did you move here?"

I shrug my shoulders.

"I asked you a question!" he barks. "In this country, you reply by speaking!"

"What was the question?" I ask.

Someone behind me laughs.

"Why. Did. You. Move. Here?" hisses Mr. Cooper.

"This is the best country in the world." My words laugh at him.

"Really? Why is that?"

I think for a second. "Teachers are easy here."

The class laughs. At him. Mr. Cooper frowns. He does not enjoy this.

"You know what, Mr. Shen? I think you were smoking something funny at lunchtime. Get up."

"Why?" The smoke makes me brave and careless.

"Because I say so."

"What if I don't?" Some girl used these words in another class.

He towers over me. "I'll grab your collar and pull you up."

"Like the police?"

"What?" Mr. Cooper's mouth hangs open in surprise.

"Like the police in China," I say. "They grab your collar, and then they slam your head into the wall. When you land on the ground, they kick you."

"Mr. Shen, get out! Your chair is waiting in the principal's office."

Chapter Four

"Hey, China!"

Is someone talking to me? I must be dreaming. I turn around and Chief is grinning at me.

"Hey, Chief!" I call out.

The two of us have never spoken before but here we are, greeting each other like brothers. In class, I took a desk far away from his. I didn't want some bigmouth saying that we looked alike.

Anyone glancing into our classroom without a careful look would think we were both Chinese.

What's he doing out here in the hallway? He should be in that socials class. Didn't the cops arrest him at the mall?

"Where're you going?" he asks.

I poke my chin toward the office. "Nowhere."

"You get under Cooper's skin?" He clowns at stroking a beard on his face. "Hey, you want to come with us? We're going to Pinhead's for a smoke."

I warn myself to stay cool. I mustn't make a fool of myself. What if they're playing a prank? They always tell lies to the teachers about why they're late. Why wouldn't they lie to me?

"Hey, we know everything." He swings an arm around my shoulder and pulls me close. He wears cologne. "We know, okay? The Man told us."

When I pull back, he repeats slowly, "The Man told us, okay? He's your dealer, right? He'll keep your secret. Us too! Okay? You got friends now, okay?"

Friends? The potheads? But they're the least friendly ones of all. Pinhead and Danny McMann are skinny as broomsticks and have stringy greasy hair. No one talks to them. They only talk to each other. Well, Danny has a girlfriend. They don't belong to any crowd. They're not in the sports group, the brains group, the cadets group or the rich group. They must have hooked up with Chief to smoke pot and to snicker at all the stupid little groups around them.

But Chief is right. I do have friends now. A newcomer like me can't be choosy.

Chief drives an old Toyota with lots of rust gnawing at the body. Pinhead sits in the front, while Danny and his girlfriend, Shawna Smith, are packed in the back with me. The sagging seats have lost all their softness and press hard against our backsides. The car reeks of beer, pot and cigarettes.

"What a surprise, eh? China smokes!"

It takes me a moment to see that Chief is talking about me. "No big deal," I say, shrugging.

"It's a rough life here, isn't it?"

Chief twists the dial on the dashboard, and the speakers blast out twanging guitars.

"Hey, China, you like country music?" he asks.

I'm not sure which country he's referring to. "I listen to music all the time."

I stare out the window. This must be the poor part of town. Torn screen doors swing from the fronts of small houses. Old paint is peeling from walls. Darkened windows look over patchy brownish lawns. A rusty tricycle lies upside down on someone's driveway. This place contains none of the lush streets of trees and pretty flowers that US TV programs showed us in China.

"I smoked all my stuff at lunch," I confess.

"Don't worry. We got lots."

A sour smell floats through Pinhead's house. It is strongest in the kitchen, so it must come from cooking. Dirty pots and dishes are piled high in the sink, along the counter and on the table.

We head downstairs, where the basement is filled by a huge pool table. It makes me think of a swimming pool, and I want to dive into the dark glowing green. I want it to be a big blob of Jell-O that will hold me up. The ceiling is low, so suddenly we all look bigger. Pinhead slides open the tiny grimy windows and starts a floor-stand fan that swivels from side to side. He turns on a boom box, and loud music thumps off the walls. It is more of that country's music, that country they just spoke about. Danny and Shawna drop onto a sofa and pull out a bag of weed.

Chief leans against the pool table. "Hey, China! You play?"

I shrug. "A little."

The others look surprised, as if they never heard of Chinese people playing pool. In Toronto, I spent far too much time at the pool hall. Ma dragged me to this small town thinking she would finally stop me from playing.

Chief racks the balls. "You break," he says.

The others come to watch. My first shot will be the big test. I lean over and slide my stick back and forth on my bridge to loosen my arm and find my balance. I hit the cue ball smack in the center. It breaks the rack with a loud crack, and the balls scatter widely, like baby chicks in a farm-yard. That should impress the potheads. Playing pool is the only thing that lifts me out of my ugly little life and lets me be a winner.

This is why I need friends. If you play for money, then you should only take cash from people you know. It can be dangerous to beat someone you don't know. What if the guy is a gangster with bodyguards waiting outside?

I walk to the side and pocket an easy one on the three ball. That makes me happy.

Solid balls have always brought me good luck when I play. There is a pureness and beauty to those balls that the striped ones lack. When they're spinning they look free and powerful.

I scratch my next shot and let Chief shoot. I want to see him play. He is good. He cuts his shot and sinks the eleven ball. Danny tries to hand me a joint, but I say no.

Chief notices and laughs. "Hey, China! Relax! You play too serious!"

I haven't decided if I want to take this game or let Chief win. He saunters around the table and lines up his next shot. He doesn't pause to think about his moves. Bang, bang, bang. He's fast. Chief sinks another ball and then another one. He wins the game, and then Pinhead wants to play me. But I shake my head and reach for a joint. I think the others are waiting to see me smoke.

When I feel relaxed, I ask, "What happened with the cops in the mall?"

"Some jerk spilled water on the floor," says Chief, blowing out a mouthful of smoke. "I slipped and my foot went out from under me. They should never have caught me. I was almost at the door. I was almost out of there!"

"Hah! You're getting fat on us," says Pinhead.

"You weren't there, you prick," retorts Chief. "What the hell do you know?"

"A lady cop cuffed you!" laughs Pinhead.

"She took down The Man," snaps Chief, "not me."

Danny joins in. "That's not what I heard."

"I was there," I say. "In the mall. She grabbed The Man, not him."

Chief throws a fake punch at Pinhead and then grins at me. "Thanks, China. You and I, we'll stick together against these white boys."

"What happened at the cop station?" Shawna sounds bored.

"I'm still a student," says Chief, bragging, "so they have to treat me as low risk. The chief of my band council meets with their youth justice group. The cops, they hate meetings."

"They hate meetings, but they love sitting on their fat asses," says Danny.

"They just love their fat asses," says Shawna.

Pinhead chortles, and soon we are all laughing. We can't stop.

Now I can tell Ma I have new friends. I can tell her I visited someone's house. I saw his basement and enjoyed a western welcome. Chips and drinks were served. Too bad Ma will hate these people. These are the very last people that she wants me to make friends with.

That makes me laugh even harder.

Chapter Five

With my new friends, I get to play more pool. I also see more of this ugly town.

Danny's place has thick lumpy rugs that look like a blanket of shiny brown slugs. In some rooms it goes halfway up the walls. Shawna lives with her mom in a small apartment. We go out and smoke on their balcony, which is stacked high with junk: bikes, a barbecue grill, paint cans, a chest of drawers and two chairs that are each missing a leg. She and Danny go to the bedroom, so Chief, Pinhead and I squeeze against one another at the railing. We see the water tower, warehouses, railway tracks and a strip mall with hardly any customers. Chief points to one of the stores and brags about his sister working there part-time.

One day I bring the potheads to my home, but only after they promise to smoke nothing but tobacco inside the house. Ma lights a cigarette every now and then, so that smell is not a problem.

At first they don't want to come.

"Let's go to your place, Chief," says Pinhead.

"Yeah, isn't it your turn?" asks Danny. "When do we get our grand tour of the reserve?"

Chief shakes his head and frowns. He owns the car, so we go wherever he decides.

"Let's go to China's," he says. "I've never been inside a Chinese house."

As he drives up to my place, I repeat, "If you want to toke up, go to the backyard. Okay?"

Inside, Shawna sniffs the air. "Nice house," she says with a smile. "Leather sofas smell so sexy."

"My dad bought it," I say.

"He has taste."

"He's a jerk."

"Where'd he go?"

"He has a new girlfriend."

"That sucks." She offers me a smoke and adds, "Is he in China?"

"Can we have a beer?" Pinhead calls from the kitchen.

He must have poked his head into the fridge. These guys are being extra polite here. At Danny's place, no one ever asks if it is okay for us to take stuff. We just go ahead and eat and drink whatever we find. We have seen everyone's home except for Chief's. So far, I have to say my house is the nicest. And I am not boasting.

Chief and Pinhead creep from the kitchen, flop onto the sofa and prop their feet on the coffee table. They marvel at the size of the home theater and play with the remote.

"What is that, a seventy-two-inch?" asks Pinhead.

"I could camp here forever," says Chief.

"Which movie do you want to watch?" Shawna is good at getting things started.

"Look at this, *Die Hard III*!" shouts Danny.

Then Ma comes in. She is home earlier than usual. Josh clings to her hand.

"Who are these people?" Her Chinese comes out low and soft, but I know she's upset.

"My friends," I reply cheerfully. "You said to invite them home."

"These...these ones cannot be your friends." She is flustered. "They...they look like hooligans!"

She rushes to the kitchen.

"What'd she say?" asks Shawna.

"She had a rough day."

"Hey, we should go." Chief pours beer down his throat as if it's a drainpipe.

"The movie just started," protests Pinhead. "I've been waiting to see this."

"Me too," says Danny. "Why don't you relax? Go get another beer."

Chief looks at Shawna. She shrugs, so he heads to the kitchen. I hope Ma has a heart attack, drops to the floor and dies. She has never spoken to a First Nations person.

A second later, she hurries through the living room. Is there a fire somewhere? I laugh to myself. I grab the remote and punch the volume as high as it can go.

When Chief doesn't come out, I wonder what's going on and go to the kitchen. He's at the table, chatting with my little brother.

"…how old are you?"

"Three," says Josh.

"You speak good English."

"Thank you. So do you."

"Where were you born?"

"Toronto."

"Do you like this country?"

"Yes."

"How come?"

"This is home!"

"*Zuo-xin*, come with me." Ma pushes past me and pulls Josh from the room.

Chief strides through the living room to the front door. "I'm outta here," he says to his pals. "If you stay, you can walk home."

I rarely see the potheads move so fast. What if I never see them again?

"Please don't bring those people here again," Ma says at dinner. "They will cause trouble."

"They're my friends," I protest.

"I want to see some books. Textbooks, not comic books."

"Our textbooks were piled in the car," I say.

"I want you to have friends who will help you study, that's all."

I mention that Chief's sister is smart enough to be on Fast-Track and will probably win scholarships for university. Ma changes the topic and asks about *Ke-rou* and *Dao-chen*, my buddies in China from years ago.

"Have they sent you e-mails recently?"

I don't answer. She never liked those two and always called them stinky eggs.

"You should tell them about your new school here," she says.

"They have girlfriends now," I mutter. "Very pretty girls."

"Your marks are better here than in China," says Ma. "Did you tell them?"

"Those four go out all the time. They have fun. They are normal people."

"You can get into college."

"*Ke-rou* has gone with several girls. He dated three at the same time."

"After college, you will earn good money."

"I'm not going to college. I told you."

"Then how will you take care of me?" She looks me in the eye. "I am a woman, all alone in a strange country."

I hate it when she plays at being a weakling. She has never been frail. Carefully, I set down my chopsticks. "Why should I take care of you? You told me to bring friends home. And then you were so rude to them. Don't you want me to have friends?"

She sighs and says firmly, "You should have the right kind of friends, that's all."

Chapter Six

Between first and second period next morning, I see Chief far down the hallway. He stands out like a stop sign in that ocean of blond heads. He struts beside Pinhead. Their bodies and long hair sway from side to side as if they are listening to music only they can hear.

I head toward them, but Chief sails by without meeting my eyes. What happened? Now I am an insect too small to be seen.

Chief's eyes usually take in all of school life. He is alert and up-to-date and never misses a thing. I am sure he resents how poorly Ma treated him yesterday.

Chief is a tough guy, but rudeness is hard for anyone to take. It must be even worse when it comes from someone new to your country. His people once owned this entire nation, but now no one respects them. In China, people hate boastful foreigners and pushy tourists. I want to apologize to Chief, but it's too late now. I have too much stubborn pride. I hate saying sorry, especially for someone else's bad manners.

Later, Chief strolls into math. His sister Diane sits at the front of the class, so of course Chief has a desk as far away as possible. She is pretty, has a nice body and knows how to look good. And because she is smart at math, the school put her on the Fast-Track program. Too bad none of the kids on Fast-Track have many friends. Here, if you do well at school, all the kids avoid you as though you have a contagious disease.

When the bell rings for lunch, Chief shoots out the door. I don't plan to follow him until I realize I'm out of stuff. Last night I finished my bundle on the way to the Always Open. Ma needed milk, and she is afraid to drive alone at night.

I run across the football field, wondering if Chief is in the trees. I'm in luck. Chief is there, sitting on a stump, alone. He's smoking a cigarette.

"Sorry about yesterday," I start.

He cuts me off. "No big deal."

I sit across from him. "You have any stuff?"

He shakes his head.

"Time to see The Man," I say.

"Be careful, China," he says. "The cops are out to nail him."

Chief seems to have forgiven me. Right away I feel better. "They always are," I sneer.

"A plainclothes cop was at school this morning," Chief tells me. "He was asking questions."

"He's wasting his time," I reply.

Chief hands over his cigarette and I inhale.

"So, China, how do you like our little town?" he asks.

"It's okay."

"Must be hard being the only China in town."

"It's okay."

"You and I might be related," he says. "Some folks say my people came from Asia, crossing the Bering Strait when it was solid land, not water."

"So now I have to let you copy my math homework?"

We laugh, even though I don't know what the Bering Strait is. Chief never talks about his people.

"We shouldn't hang out together," he says.

"Why not?" I fight off the urge to run. If he doesn't want me here, I won't beg for his company. I'm not that pitiful.

"No ghetto for me," he declares.

"No what?" I don't know the word.

"Ghetto. It's a slum, a dump for the non-whites."

"I don't live in a dump," I say, offended.

"I'm kidding, idiot!" He leans forward and lightly taps my cheek with his fingers.

I smile weakly. Western jokes are very hard to figure out.

"How's Celine?" he asks.

I shrug.

"Aren't you two an item?"

"Are you crazy? She's not my type."

In truth, I have thought about her. Many times. I don't even notice, but suddenly I will be daydreaming about her. At school, at the deli, on the street. Celine is easy to be with. When she talks to me, it's like her mind is completely focused. I think she can see into my soul, and I want to tell her every little detail about my life. I want to be close to her, real close. I try to breathe in her perfume, to get as much of her inside me as possible. Both Chief and I are lost in thought, dreaming about Celine. Can you imagine? The two biggest losers in the school are chasing the girl most likely to succeed.

Pinhead rushes up. He is bug-eyed. "Did you hear? Danny and Shawna got hauled into the office. A plainclothes cop asked them a whole bunch of questions about The Man. And then Danny got taken to the police station!"

I jump up to see if anyone is following Pinhead. The last thing I need is trouble with the cops. But I can't run off right away. I would look like a coward. Pinhead should not have come running. It would make cops and teachers notice him.

Pinhead is bent over, panting and gasping. "Shawna's mom came and took her home," Pinhead adds. "She looked mad!"

"Ah, Danny will be fine." Chief shrugs. "Nothing will happen."

"They took him to the station!"

"They're just trying to scare him. Listen, this is what they'll do. They'll write down Danny's birthdate. They'll take his fingerprints. They'll talk really slowly and seriously. They'll even take his photo. But nothing will happen."

Pinhead looks at me. "You better get lost. You don't want to be seen with us. The cops will grab you next."

"Maybe I should go." I try not to sound too eager.

"Don't worry," Chief says. "You're new here, right? And you're from China. The cops won't bother you. They're afraid they'll be called racist."

"Can you give me some stuff?" I ask Pinhead.

"Are you kidding? I just flushed everything I had down the toilet!"

"There's nothing to worry about." Chief laughs.

I'm not so sure. Cops have power, and they like to use it. And the people of this law-and-order town want to know their police are strong and fearless.

Chapter Seven

Next day in homeroom, Mr. Grant asks if anyone has seen Danny. "Is the little pest coming back? Have they shipped him off to jail? Or have they shaved his head and made him respectable?"

The kids ignore him like a puddle of vomit on the sidewalk.

I eat lunch by myself and keep a safe distance from Shawna, Chief and Pinhead.

I doubt that any student here would snitch on us. I don't know the kids at this school, but I do know this: they all hate the police. In this town, the police don't look anything like the handsome stars you see on TV. Those ones must all be stationed in the big cities where real life happens.

Here the cops are middle-aged and fat from sitting all day in the donut shop. If kids hang around the food court at the mall with no purchased food in front of them, an officer will order them to move along, move along. No exceptions, not even for the ones who have books open in front of them and claim to be doing homework.

The next day, Danny shows up just as the bell rings. A grin snakes across his face. The kids surround his desk to ask what happened at the police station.

"Nothing." He leans back and props his feet on a table. "They took down my ID, they took my fingerprints and they took my photo. But they didn't charge me."

"Did they have a cell waiting for you?" asks someone.

"Had my own!"

"Not a cell phone, stupid. A jail cell."

It sounds like the police are starting a file on him. They will be following him, watching him and adding more notes and details to the file. They'll set a trap for him one day. Who knows who else they will catch next.

When I glance up, the kids are staring at me. To them, I am already tied up in front of a firing squad, a blindfold over my eyes. I look away, out the window. They've seen me hanging out with Chief and Danny and Pinhead. They know I'm a pothead.

Later that morning, Celine stops me in the hallway. I'm surprised because the last time we talked was a long time ago, back in September. She smiles and I notice she is wearing a new shade of lipstick, something grayish pink.

"Hey, how are things going?" she asks.

Other kids turn to look, puzzled that she is talking to garbage like me. Suddenly I feel I'm ten feet tall. I also wonder if she might be spying for the cops. Her mother is a lawyer, right?

"Fine," I say. Isn't she finished with her good deed, showing me around school? Once I joined the potheads, I didn't think she would talk to me.

"Need help with any homework?" she asks.

I shake my head. I don't want to owe her any favors. She was *told* to help the new student. She really didn't want to be with me.

"I was wondering if you could help me out." She moves in closer because she lowers her voice. She doesn't want nearby students to hear. "Can you ask Chief if he could show me around the reserve? I want to shoot some video there. I need some footage for my history project."

"Why don't you ask him yourself?" I ask.

Her face reddens a bit. "They don't like white people going through the reserve," she tells me. "You're his friend. He'll say yes to you but no to me."

"I don't know," I reply. But I want to pay off my debt to her. "I'll ask him later today."

"Great! Thanks a lot, Jason. You're a great guy."

This time, her smile swallows me up.

My eyes follow the sway of her tight jeans as she hurries away. I sure hope Chief says yes. It would be nice if she owed me a favor. If she were my friend, I might even stop my crazy smoking.

"No way!" Chief shoots a lungful of smoke high into the air. "I'd rather jump off the water tower than help her."

He pulls long and hard at his cigarette. The end burns bright orange, and it shrinks and shrivels right in front of my eyes. We sit at the far end of the field. The football team is running drills, back and forth across the green grass. From time to time we hear them yell out hearty chants to keep up their energy.

"Why not?" I ask.

"If she gets out there, she'll want to fix this and fix that, start writing letters and make lots of trouble."

I frown. "Last time her name came up, you were okay."

"That was then."

"She helped me," I add hopefully.

"Then she's your problem."

"She just wants to look around the reserve," I plead.

"That place is private property," says Chief.

"What's the big deal?" I ask. "Everyone has to live somewhere."

"Nobody goes there," he declares. "Not my friends and for sure not my enemies."

"She says she's doing a school project."

"No! She wants to use the reserve to win herself an A. No way will anyone exploit my people again. Especially her."

Chief clenches his fists and looks ready to punch me senseless. If it were anyone else, I would back off, I would be long gone. But Chief is supposed to be a friend.

So I ask a tough question. "Is it because she's white?"

"Maybe."

"Doesn't that make you racist?"

"Shut up!"

"All I said was—"

He doesn't let me finish. "You don't know what the hell you're talking about."

I do know. And when people tell me to shut up, that's when I'll speak up. "Listen, people may not want to buy coffee from me because I smell bad or because my coffee tastes bitter. That's okay. I can change those things. But it's not okay if they stay away because I'm Chinese."

"Look who's talking," he sneers. "You never even looked at me until I went up to you to talk."

"I didn't talk to *anyone*," I protest. "No one ever said hi."

"You're new here. You just got into town. What did you expect? Everyone has to *earn* respect, you know."

"That's crap," I say. "And you know it."

Chapter Eight

Every few days or so, I sneak into Ma's purse. Inside, there's a packet of cash from the day's sales at the deli. I'll lift one or two twenty-dollar bills, depending on how much she has. I save all my pickings for trips to buy goods from The Man.

I have stolen her money many times before, but tonight things don't go smoothly. Sometimes I think bad luck follows me no matter where I go, no matter what I do. Ma throws her purse onto the bed, so I wait until she goes to the bathroom. Then I tiptoe into her room.

This time, just as I open the bag, I hear Josh's voice. "Ma says don't ever touch her purse."

I freeze. If I warn him not to tell, even under the threat of locking him in the ghost room in the basement, for sure he will run straight to Ma and blab. So I choose my words with care.

"Ma told me to take this." I wave a bill in his face before stuffing it into my pocket. "For school."

"I didn't hear you ask."

"You were watching TV, stupid. You think you know everything? You think you're running this household?"

Then I saunter off.

We are about to start dinner when Ma drops her chopsticks with a clatter. She props her elbows on the table and rubs her eyes. "I don't know what this rotten world is coming to!" She sounds like she is in pain.

I freeze. Did Josh open his big mouth?

"The mall is raising our rent by five percent," she says. "And another deli is opening up where the shoe repair store used to be."

Relieved, I reach for some food.

"Worst of all," she continues, "the new deli owners are immigrants from China too. They are the fiercest rivals any merchant can have. For sure they will beat our prices. I don't know how I can feed this family."

"It's time to go back to China," I declare. "More people live there, so any store there has a better chance of success. In this dinky little town, of course it's tough."

"If I can find a small apartment to rent, we'll move," Ma says.

"In China we would be among our own people," I say.

"We have to save money wherever we can," Ma declares.

She's not listening to me. Yet she's always complaining that I don't listen to her.

"Everything is cheaper in China," I insist. "Why stay here if you want to save money?"

"Maybe we can sell that stupid home theater," she muses. "Too bad it's already out-of-date."

Finally she looks at me. "No more expensive running shoes," she says. "Don't try to argue with me."

She's going to go into the city, stop in Chinatown and buy the cheapest shoes there. They're ugly and everyone knows they are low-end knockoffs. I won't wear them!

"Can't you ask Ba for some money?" I demand. He sends her a check every month.

She glares at me. She won't talk to Ba if she can help it.

When I look at Josh, tears are streaming down his face. Too bad Ma doesn't notice. Hey, she's out to hammer me. I'm the number one son, so therefore I'm also the number one target.

"Maybe you can get a part-time job," she continues. "You can learn better English in a different store."

"No one else will work for you for free," I retort. "You will lose even more money."

"Mei has offered to help. Maybe you don't need that cell phone of yours," she says. "No one ever calls you."

That's when I leave the table. I slam the door to my room and bounce onto the bed. I curse at the ceiling. When Ma's life gets flushed down the toilet in a loud swoosh, so does mine. Less money in Ma's purse means less cash I can take. Lately I need more funds than before because of the potheads. It feels good to have friends, to have pals. They are smiling and laughing, and we are getting high together. I can count on them.

What am I going to do? If Ma cuts my cell phone account, I will be the worst geek at school. Even if no one ever calls me, I can flip open my cell and press the keypad and look busy. Now I may as well hang myself.

Can my life get any uglier?

When I told Celine that Chief said no about taking her to the reserve, she shrugged. "Fine. It's a free country, right?"

She dashed off before I could say anything. It felt as if it was my fault that Chief had said no.

I have a little money hidden away, and right now I could use a puff. But where do I get the stuff? Ever since the police showed up at school, The Man doesn't keep regular hours at any of his former stops. No one can find him.

I wish Chief would phone and say he's driving into town and calling all the potheads to hang out together. He always has neat things to say and can make us all laugh. But we've avoided each other these past few days.

Later that night, my cell rings. Ma is in the kitchen. I rush in and wave the phone at her. "Hear this? It's my cell ringing! It's my friends calling! Are you saying you don't want me to have friends?"

"Hey, China," says Chief. "Are you cool?"

"Always," I reply. "And you?"

"You got any spare cash on you?" he asks.

"A couple of bills."

"I hear The Man is in town," he says, "but only for tonight. Pinhead would go, but he's flat broke. Can you get us some stuff?"

"Where will he be?" I want to ask if it's safe, but who wants to sound stupid?

"Not far from you, at the Always Open."

"Parking lot?" I ask.

"Where else?"

Chapter Nine

I'm walking on Main Street, the busy road that winds through Milson and connects to the highway. When I see the Always Open ahead, I cross to the other side and slow down. This way I can better check out the place. The cops might be around, right?

Dusk is falling, so streetlamps and store signs provide the light. But it's wasted because there's not a single human on the street. People in this town take their cars everywhere, even though they are the world's worst drivers. The other stores in the strip mall have closed for the night, so all their parking spots are empty.

What's in front of the Always Open? A rusty old van painted with the store's logo, a station wagon with a woman in the front seat and several children bouncing around in the back, and a big black SUV floating on oversized tires. The Man drives rented cars to make it harder for the cops to follow him. Every time I meet him, he is driving something different. But it is always brand-new and always a big American tank. Maybe this isn't the best time to be meeting The Man, seeing that the cops are after him.

I go inside and grab a plastic basket. I drop in two bags of potato chips, a pack of M&M's and some ginger ale. Ma asked me to get milk, again, and some eggs. Then I check the new magazines on the rack. From time to time I glance out at the parking lot. The potheads will owe me big tonight, after I deliver the goods. Whenever they are broke, which seems like a lot of the time, they borrow money from me. Tonight they're getting free delivery too.

A long shiny car pulls up. The Man enters the Always Open and looks around. He's wearing a baseball hat and the usual oversized jacket. He buys a bottle of water and goes out. I pay for my things and leave. He has lit a cigarette and leans against the lamppost, watching the stream of stop-and-start traffic on Main Street.

I peer around the corner of the building to see if someone might be hiding there. I kneel and pretend to be tying my shoelace.

"Nice night, eh?" He doesn't even look at me.

"Three bags." I speak out of the side of my mouth.

"So much?"

I stand up. "I'm buying for my friends."

"You bring bling?

I trust him, otherwise I wouldn't be here, so the cash goes over, and he licks his fingers to start the count.

He drops the pot into my bag, and I turn to leave. But the doors of the rusty van fly open and two men jump out, guns drawn.

"Don't move!" they shout.

Cops! I dash to the corner, but a goon there grabs my arm, twists it and slams me to the wall. "Where're you going?" he grunts.

He cuffs my wrists and hands my bag to his backup. "Check this out," he calls.

"Whoa," says his friend.

"We'll nail this one for trafficking. He was buying for friends."

A police cruiser pulls up, sirens blaring and red-blue lights flashing. I get thrown into the backseat. A crowd is gawking at us. Where the hell did all these nosy baboons come from? Don't they have reality TV shows to watch at home?

At the station, they march me into a room that holds nothing but a table and three hard chairs. They ask questions and record my answers. The room smells of coffee, but there's nothing to drink. What's my name, age, address? Do I know Daniel McMann and Winston Hedley? Winston who? Turns out that is Pinhead's real name. What was I doing at the Always Open tonight?

"I went to buy some snacks."

"Have you met this man before?" They shove a photo of The Man at me.

I shake my head.

"Really? We saw you give him a big bundle of bills."

"My friends told me they were buying cell phones from him. That's what I thought he put into my bag."

"How many cell phones did you think you were buying?"

"Three."

"Now you're saying you went to the store to buy cell phones for your pals. At first you said you went to buy some snacks."

Words leap from my mouth. "I told Pinhead I was getting snacks, so he asked me to pick up the cell phones."

Wow! My brain surges with a life of its own! It's a miracle!

"Hey, kid, do you smoke pot?" The cop leans against the wall, watching me closely.

"I don't tell lies," I tell them. And then I add, "So, yeah, I've smoked. Just a few times, with the kids at school. So what? Hey, everyone at school smokes."

"That's crap," he snaps. "Hardly anyone smokes."

What planet has he been living on? The potheads are the serious smokers, but other kids take a whiff now and then too.

Another cop comes in and slides a sheet of paper at me. "This is your statement," he says. "Read it, and if it says what you told us tonight, sign at the bottom."

"Aren't you going to let me go?"

"No, we're laying charges."

"But those other times, you let Chief and Danny go!" Wait a minute! Panic explodes in me. This isn't supposed to happen! "Those guys were my friends. This is all the same thing!"

"You're going to court to see the judge," says the cop.

"Chief and Danny?" says the other. "Oh, we made a mistake there. Jason Shen, you are under arrest. You are charged with possession of marijuana for the purpose of trafficking. Do you want to talk to a lawyer?"

This cannot be happening. This is a bad dream. But I don't let anything show on my face. I look at the door. Can I get out before they grab me again?

"Hey, kid, you want to talk to your parents?"

"If the judge finds me guilty," I ask, "will I have to go to jail?"

"All up to the judge," says the cop. "Maximum sentence for trafficking is five years. Hey, kid, you got caught with the goods right in your hot little hands. We've been watching The Man for years. You better get a good lawyer."

Chapter Ten

Ma drives me home. She doesn't say a word, as if I'm not there. I glance at her. The glare from the streetlamps makes her look old and yellow. In the backseat, Josh knows something is wrong. He doesn't make a sound.

Inside the house, I run to my room and clamp on headphones and crank the music as high as it can go. But there's no escaping my thoughts.

and make lots of noise. That would ma
it easier for me to walk out on her.

"There is one handy thing about y
going to jail," she says. "I won't need
buy so much food. With only two of u
Josh and I can move in with Aunt Mei. W
can save our rent money. Just think, yo
will be fed and housed and clothed by the
state. I am so lucky!"

I fold my arms over my chest and look
away. Get on with it, my mind shouts,
hurry up and get it over!

"What shall I tell your Ba?" she
demands. "This should make him happy.
He can curse me as a useless mother, as a
giant failure. He will say that none of this
would have happened if you had followed
him instead of me."

She is trying to make me feel guilty,
ut I don't fall into her trap. All this
uble happened for a reason, and she is
one to blame. She brought me here.
dn't want to come here. Not even for
a second.

Ma will be angry. She will pick up
heavy things and throw them at me. Her
aim is bad, and she will dent the walls
instead. She will scream foul names at me.
She will demand to know why I would do
such a thing. As if she can ever understand
me. But she won't hit me or kick me or
slam me against the wall. That's what Ba
used to do. Of course now she will claim
she should have beaten me more often.
A good thrashing might have driven some
common sense into me.

I plan to fling this at her: "I told you
I hated it here. Over and over I said so.
I wanted to go back to China. But you
never listened. All this is your fault."

Or these words: "If you hadn't asked
me to get milk from the store, this would
never have happened. This is what I get
for being helpful!"

Right now I need something to soften
the fear biting into me. But there is nothing
on hand.

After a while, I wonder why Ma hasn't
stormed in here to yell at me. Is she

gathering her strength, whipping herself into a crazed frenzy? In the living room, Josh is watching TV.

"Where's Ma?" I ask.

"Don't know. I came out when I heard the front door."

The front door isn't locked. That's not how Ma wants it. I go to the kitchen. There's nothing to eat. My potato chips were kept by the cops. Jerks! They're likely wolfing them down right now. I glance at the clock. She has been gone almost an hour. Should I be worried?

I phone Aunt Mei and ask if Ma is at her place.

"No," she replies. "Did she go out?"

I hang up before she throws me more stupid questions.

I turn off the TV and order Josh back to bed. He whines and pulls out his bag of delaying tricks. At last he goes. I hope Ma hasn't done something stupid, like go down to the railway tracks and wait for the engine to pass. I hope she won't hurt herself. I've gone there sometimes late at night too, but I always come back. Maybe she's driven off to the city, heading to the airport to buy a ticket that will fly her to China. Hey, wait a minute. I'm the one who needs to go there, not her.

When Ma comes in, her arms are wrapped tight around herself. She didn't take a sweater or jacket. She marches to the kitchen, her gaze firmly fixed on the ground. It's good she returned home, but I don't show any feelings. I turn on the TV but it's too much noise and flash. I pick up the newspaper, but the print keeps dancing out of focus.

Ma brings two mugs of hot tea. She and sinks into the sofa, hugging a c in her hands. Dark bags hang und swollen eyes.

"I'm not angry anymore." Sh

"If I had stayed here, I mi grabbed the kitchen knife and And then I would go to jail. that?"

She should be more raging anger. She shoul

"What should I do?" she asks. "I can walk out the door and then you and your brother will never see me again. What should I do? You tell me, *Jie-xin*. You're old enough to do what you want. You're old enough to hold opinions."

"You should keep working," I grunt. "Find a new husband. Have another baby. You still have a life."

I say this only to push the talking along. She can lash out and scream at me for bringing down the family, casting it into a deep pit of shame. She will cry out that no matter how hard she works, it all ends up as nothing. She will repeat herself, over and over. Then I can go to bed and shut my eyes and forget everything.

"What did you say to Josh?" she asks.

"Nothing."

"Don't tell him any of this."

"When I go to jail," I sneer, "he will see that I'm not home for dinner. He's not that stupid."

"Do we need to hire a lawyer?"

"No." All of a sudden, the path ahead is clear for me. "I'm going to tell the judge I am guilty. It's all very simple. I broke the law and should be punished."

I feel big and brave saying this. I will protect my friends. But the strength lasts only for a second. Then I want to thrust my fist through the TV screen.

"You can blame me for all this," Ma says, catching me by surprise.

Her voice cracks. "I should have taken action long ago. I knew you were stealing money from my purse. I knew you smoked that stuff. I knew you might get into trouble. But I kept waiting, hoping you would see right from wrong. I thought you would straighten out yourself."

She bursts into tears.

"Ma, let me go back to China," I say. "Let me go before I get sent to jail. Wouldn't you rather have me in China than in jail?"

She keeps crying, and I start to feel bad. "I was stupid this time," I finally admit, staring at my feet. "Really stupid. I know it now. So won't you help me?"

Chapter Eleven

My new career is full-time nanny. The school suspends me because the drug charge is so heavy. Parents worry that I might sell pot to their darling children, so they complain to the principal. Ma tells me to stay away from her deli because the whole town knows about my disgrace. She will have to work extra hard to keep her customers. They should feel sorry for her because she is a single mom.

Josh knows I'm in big trouble, yet he tugs me to watch TV beside him. He wants to be let outside. He begs me to play video games. He nags me to cook instant noodles for him. I shut my bedroom door, but still he charges in.

I can't go to school for two weeks, but I'm supposed to keep studying. Yeah, right. I'm going to win a million dollars in the lottery too. All I've done is watch every rental movie from the Always Open, some twice or three times. I always click on the English subtitles if they are available. Then it looks like I'm working on my English.

There is a knock. Josh runs ahead of me to the front door.

"Hey, Little China," Chief calls out. "Remember me?"

"You're not supposed to be here," I say halfheartedly. The police ordered me to stay away from the potheads until after my trial.

"You shouldn't be here either, China," he replies.

He's the rat who sent me to the Always Open that night. He's no friend. Why can't he leave me alone? Shouldn't he be at school?

"Let's go for a ride," he says.

"Can't." I start to shut the door. "I'm looking after my brother."

"Bring him along," says Chief. "I'm a safe driver."

"My mother would kill me."

"Who's going to know? You scared of your mother?"

Me? Never!

"You want a donut?" I ask Josh.

"Yes!" His eyes light up. Ma doesn't sell donuts at the deli, so he always wants them.

"Then don't tell anyone," I tell my brother.

At the Donut King, I order a large coffee and four triple chocolates. Josh gets a carton of chocolate milk, his favorite. Then we carry our food to sit on the grass by the railway tracks.

"Those damn cops shouldn't give you such a hard time," says Chief, sipping his coffee. "They could have let you go home with just a warning. I never heard of them charging someone on their first time."

I shrug. "They don't like Chinese."

"That sucks," says Chief.

"They found too much stuff in my bag."

"That's my fault."

"Thanks, but you get special treatment because you're First Nations," I say. "Immigrants are the last ones to arrive here, so no one respects us."

Chief tells me The Man is worse off than me. He's sitting in jail. He didn't make bail. But his trial will have nothing to do with mine. I'm going to Youth Court.

"I'm pleading guilty," I tell Chief. "That way they won't ask questions."

"Don't worry, the judge won't do anything," he says. "He'll let you off easy."

What the hell does he know? He's the one who said nothing would happen to me.

"Fight back, China. Don't let the cops walk all over you," he says. "Get a lawyer. Isn't Celine's mother a lawyer?"

"The cops want to make an example of me," I point out. "They've been trying to arrest someone for a long time."

From far away comes the steady hum of a train.

"Even more reason to fight back!" declares Chief. "You're under eighteen, so they have to use youth rules. This is your first time, and you're an okay student, right?"

"The cops want to be heroes," I say. "They want people to think crime is under control here."

He shakes his head. "Man, you got to learn to fly sometime."

"Fly what?" I don't get it.

"You, China," he says, "you need to look up instead of down. You need something pure, like the sky is sometimes."

I shrug.

A railway crossing gate swings across the road, red lights begin to flash and a bell beats out a warning. I've never seen the morning train. The potheads usually come here in the afternoon. We jump around and make faces at the passengers. We hurl rocks at the freight cars. I often wish the train would whisk me far away.

"The last thing you want is a police record," Chief warns. "It'll stay with you all your life. You'll never get a good job."

I hand Josh my last donut and push him to Chief. The horn from the train blares out shrill and long. The clattering roar gets so loud we can't hear ourselves.

The train swings around the curve. Its one headlight races toward us. High on the engine's nose, a window glints. The ground is shaking. I watch the train. It comes closer and closer. I dash to the tracks, watching a fence on the other side. Noise and wind swallow me. I jump across the front of the train.

I land on one foot and fall to the ground. Something hurts. Good, I deserve it. I should be smashed into pieces.

I pull my knees to my chest as the train hurtles by, inches from my back.

When the last car clanks by, Chief comes running. He drags Josh along by the collar. Josh is crying. His face is streaked with chocolate.

Chief pulls me up and slams me against a post. Pain twists through my back but I don't care. I hang there limply.

"You stupid bastard!" he screams. "What the hell were you doing?"

I turn away, but he slaps me hard and yanks my face back to his. "You stupid son of a bitch!" he shouts. "You almost killed yourself!"

His hands tighten at my neck and shake me like I'm a young tree. He curses and spits foul names at my face. I can't breathe. I sputter and choke. I tear at his hands, but he is much stronger. Dimly I hear Josh wailing my name.

What's going on? What's Chief upset about? He's not going to jail.

My hands clench each other. My feet grope for footing. I throw my fists up hard.

They catch Chief under the chin and knock him back. I ram my elbows out and break his grip. My lungs grab air in greedy gulps.

Chief lunges at me and throws me down. Before I can get up, he's kicking at me, over and over. I bring my arms and legs into myself, praying for him to kill me. I deserve to die.

"Don't do that crap around me," he hisses at me. "It's no joke!"

Chapter Twelve

When Chief's old Camry turns onto our street, I see Ma's car in our driveway. It shouldn't be there. Another brand-new car is parked behind it. We have guests. Maybe they can divert Ma's fury away from my little field trip. I doubt it. When I jump from the car, I don't bother saying good-bye to Chief. He can go to hell.

Inside the house, I swear softly. The day is diving from bad to worse. It's my father, wearing dress slacks, sports jacket and his smug know-it-all look. He is up to no good. He brought along his new wife. And his new son. If I had known Ba was here, I wouldn't have come in. Whenever he is late sending money to us, Ma worries that he may have gone back to China.

"See, I told you the boys would be back shortly," Ma exclaims.

Her face is tight, but she tries to sound cheerful and casual. They must have been alarmed at coming in and finding the house empty. Then Ba probably accused Ma of having no control over me. He always claimed she was too soft a mother. He thinks she should have beaten me in my younger days.

"Say hello to Aunty," Ma says. No doubt she wants us to look good in front of the new wife.

We mumble something. The woman is cuter and younger than Ma. She pushes her little boy forward but he doesn't want to come. "This is Kai," she says proudly.

The kettle starts whistling in the kitchen, and Ma hurries to make tea. Josh runs after her.

Ba clenches his jaw. I'm as tall as he is now, but he will never admit it. Still, his face is handsome behind expensive glasses. Maybe at last he's going to a hair-stylist instead of a five-dollar barber. He walks to the window and points. "Did you see my new car? German!"

"Why did you come?" My words are rude, but there's no time for polite chit-chat with him.

Ba frowns and replies bluntly, "To say good-bye."

"Ah, you've heard?" I spread my arms out and bow grandly to Ba and his perfect family. "Yes, I'm a drug dealer! Yes, I'm going to jail! Isn't that good news? Now you won't need to worry about me."

"You should have followed me and not your mother." Ba's face is grim. "If you had, you wouldn't be in all this trouble."

He holds out the ashtray to his wife. "Look, that woman still smokes. She'll ruin Josh's health."

"Aren't you still smoking?" I challenge my father.

"I stopped a year ago," he says, smirking.

He's trying to make me shoot off my mouth so that I'll make Ma look bad, but I don't fall for his trick.

Ma brings cups of tea and a plate of sweets.

"Come, come, drink something," she calls out. "You drove such a long way, you must be tired. Kai, this is the best cookie you will ever taste! Your aunty made it herself!"

I turn to leave the room, but Ba grabs my arm and hands me an envelope. It is full of large bills. It's heavy, maybe three or four thousand bucks. I glance at Ma. She shrugs tiredly at me.

"Your mother says you want to go back to China," Ba says. "You can go live with your grandfather. He will enjoy having you around."

I can't believe this! My dream come true. At the best possible time. Ba really is my father. He can be good. He saved my life. Now I owe him big. If only I hadn't been so rude at first.

"Thank you." I bow my head and speak humbly. I turn to his wife and thank her too. I'm so happy I want to grab Kai and thank him too.

I finally speak the word my father has wanted to hear from me. "Ba," I say. "Ba, I'll repay you. I promise. I'll get a job in China and send you the money."

He snorts. Of course he doesn't believe me. "I didn't give the money to your mother because I wanted to make sure you got it," he says. "That's why we drove all the way out here."

Ma puts up one hand. "I'm not arguing with anyone," she says sweetly. "Sister-in-law, you must try this tart. It is very light."

I invite my father to sit. "So, how's your work going?"

After the visitors leave, Ma sniffs, "Who would have thought your father had so much money? Who knew he was doing so well? A German car!"

"Maybe he'll give you more cash too."

"I don't want it," she says. "I'll stand on my own two feet."

I wish she would soften up. I feel bad, taking money from the man whom Ma hates most of all. She has looked after me all my life, and here, at the first sign of trouble, I go running back to my father. Am I the world's biggest traitor or what?

Ma stops at the front door. "I have to go back to work now," she says. "I will only state this once, so you listen good. The choice is yours. You can use your father's money and buy an airplane ticket and go back to China. Or you can stay, put the money in the bank, and go see the judge to face the results of your bad choices. Your father put that money in your hands, so you have to make the choice. You are old enough to think for yourself."

What is she, crazy? I never wanted to come to this country. And I have always wanted to go back to China. Always. From the very day we landed here. It was Ba who wanted to come here, and then she followed him. I didn't have a choice then, but I do now.

Now I'm going back to where I was four years ago. It wasn't that long ago, was it? I can pick up where I left off, can't I? My friends will be glad to see me. We'll go to Eat Street and feast ourselves. We'll go to concerts where I can understand the lyrics. My buddies will hook me up with a girlfriend and we'll hang out and party on Nanjing Road.

"*Ge-ge*." Josh uses the term for "elder brother." "Are you really going to China?"

It hits me then that leaving will not be easy. But I still must go.

Chapter Thirteen

One morning, halfway through *Spiderman II*, my cell phone rings. It's Danny.

"Bad news, China."

I hate it when Danny calls me China. It's okay for Chief to use that name, but only him. He started it, right?

"Diane's dead."

"Who?" I don't know anyone by that name.

"Chief's sister. The one on Fast-Track."

"What?" I don't believe him. She's too young!

"She OD'd. But no one knows if it was an accident or a suicide."

Shawna, not Danny, wants to go visit Chief. It's her mom's day off, so she took the car and told Danny to call me. I'm curious to see the reserve. When people mention it, they roll their eyes and shake their heads, as if that place is nothing but bad news. Yet at school we learn that the First Nations people are important.

I phone Ma and tell her I need to go out. "What should I do with Josh?" I ask

"Where are you going?" she demands. She talks while serving a customer.

"To see my friend Chief," I reply.

"The police told you to stay away from him."

"Some trouble came up for him."

"So?"

"His sister just died."

"Ah, that's terrible!" she exclaims. "Of course you must go see him."

When I bring Josh to the deli, Ma hands me a box of pastries to take with me. People are lined up in front of the counter, so I ask, "What will you do with Josh?"

She gives me a strange look, as if I had asked a stupid question. "The lady at the shoe store will look after him. Don't worry about us. Go see your friend."

Shawna takes Main Street out of town but doesn't turn onto the highway. Nobody says much and the radio stays off. Danny slouches down in his seat. I can tell he doesn't want to be here. I ask Shawna if Diane was her friend. It turns out they didn't know each other. Danny pulls out his cigarettes, but Shawna reminds him that it's her mom's car.

When the car flies over a big bump and starts to bounce along an unpaved road, Danny shouts, "Now we're on Native land!"

The road has potholes and puddles. Deep ruts from heavy wheels are carved into the ground. Many times my head hits the car roof. Both sides of the road are sliding into the ditches, so one car takes up what's left of the two lanes.

Once we reach a gathering of houses, Shawna gets out to ask around for Chief's home because we don't have an address. Children run away from her. We see no street signs or lampposts. Trailer homes and other half-finished houses stand here and there. The unpainted wood looks faded and worn, as if the wait for paint has been long and may never end. There are no sidewalks.

Shawna finally finds someone who tells us where to go. When we drive up to Chief's house and step from the car, people emerge from their houses to watch us. We must be an interesting group—a blond, a redhead and a Chinese are likely an unusual sight on the reserve.

A new-looking electric stove sits on the porch. I wonder if it is plugged in.

Chief opens the door and scowls at us. "What the hell do you guys want?"

How can he be so rude? We should turn around and leave.

Shawna hugs him tightly. Her long hair falls forward, and it looks as if she is draping a golden veil over Chief. Good thing she's big and tall, so Chief doesn't need to bend down.

"I'm so, so sorry," Shawna murmurs. "It must be awful for you and your folks."

Chief squeezes his eyes shut. A tear seeps from the corner of his eye.

Shawna lets go and Danny steps up. He shakes Chief's hand solemnly, as if they are adult men doing business. "This really sucks, man," he says.

I feel like a complete jerk. What do I say? I give him the pastries. I shake his hand and pat his shoulder with my other hand. Chief is tanned, but today his face looks pale and colorless. His eyes are swollen, and the skin under his nose has been rubbed raw.

"You want to meet my folks?" he asks.

Danny and Shawna glance at each other. We don't feel welcome out here.

Finally Shawna speaks softly. "You tell us, Chief. You know best."

He looks lost, lost in thought, lost in big feelings. Then he sighs. "Come on in. It'll be good for them."

I stop inside the door. "Take off my shoes?" I ask.

"Are you kidding?" scoffs Chief.

His father is a bigger older version of Chief but looks as young as the men who pass through the mall carrying young children. His eyes are sunk deep into his face behind gold-rimmed glasses. Chief's mother is slim and slight, with short curly hair. I only saw Diane from a distance, but if she grew up to look like her mother, she would have been gorgeous.

Shawna impresses me. She walks to the sofa and leans forward to shake their hands. "I'm a friend of Charles," she says. "We felt terrible when we heard the news, and we came to make sure everyone is okay."

"Thank you for coming," says the father. "This means a lot to us."

"Yes," whispers the mother. "It does."

Danny goes up and says he's really sorry to hear such bad news. I more or less repeat his words. The parents nod at us and try to smile.

Kitchen chairs have been pulled into the tiny living room, where there is only a sagging sofa and a cabinet for the TV and stereo. The top shelf is full of shiny trophies with little sports figures posing on the tops. On the walls are school pictures of Chief and his sister when they were younger. Other people are visiting the family. They look at us but do not say a word. And they don't make room for us to sit.

We head for the door, and Chief walks us to the car.

"Hey, man, are you going to be okay?" asks Danny.

"Don't know." Chief looks away, into the distance. "This is all so...weird."

"Give it time," Shawna says. "Slowly the pain will go away."

Chief shakes his head viciously, as if to fling off the gloom hanging over him. He starts to say something but stops and looks away. I look away too.

They hug and say good-bye. Shawna and Danny get into the car.

Chief turns to me. "Hey, China, did you get a lawyer yet?"

"No." I tell him about the money from my father and going back to China.

"Hey, you should stay." He frowns at me. "This is the best country in the world."

I shake my head. "Not for me."

"I need company," he says.

"You have company," I say. "You've got Danny, Shawna and Pinhead. You've known them longer than me."

"They're white," Chief says. "You're not."

Chapter Fourteen

I don't know if Shawna or Danny went to the funeral. They didn't call me, and I'm not allowed to call anyone. In truth I was relieved. I wouldn't have known how to act. I've never gone to a funeral, here or in China. I'm not sure if that's a good thing or not. All I know is that everyone wears dark clothing and looks awful.

When I get back to school after the suspension, my life is like it was before I met Chief. No one talks to me. Kids are afraid of being dragged into court along with me. Who wants a criminal record? Now the teachers give me dirty looks too.

I'm counting off the days until my flight to China. I have bought the air ticket, and the visa will be ready in a few days. If the cops here won't treat me fairly, I have no choice but to leave.

Chief doesn't show up for classes. He must still feel sad about his sister. Poor guy. As much as I don't like my little brother, I would feel bad if anything happened to him. Most of all, I would feel awful for Ma. Parents should never see their child die. It's not right. Older people are supposed to die first.

Early one morning, Pinhead phones me. He wakes me up. He's lucky I pick up his call. He asks if I've seen Chief. He says Chief's mom is phoning all his friends, trying to find him. He hasn't been home for two nights. Pinhead asks me to walk over to the Always Open and see if Chief might be there. I leave the house right away. It is still dark.

A light rain is falling and the air is cool as I jog down Main Street. The store is empty. I go around to the covered loading bay. He's not there. There are a million places to look, and I would need a car to check every spot. I head home, thinking to get my bike.

Chief might have gone to the railway tracks or Donut King. Or he might have gone to the bandstand in the park. He could stay dry there. Through the drizzle I see the water tower, looming big and white against the gray sky. The town's name is printed in huge block letters. Suddenly I recall the words he said to me: *You got to learn to fly, man.*

Chief and Pinhead and Danny have bragged about climbing the water tower, but I've never done it.

I splash through puddles, and the cold damp crashes against me. Cars zoom by.

Drivers must think I'm just some early-morning fitness freak.

Chief has never complained about being Native, but it can't be easy. People at the mall won't sit near the First Nations people. Ma's customers complain about taxpayers' money being given to them. An invisible line divides them from everybody else. Both sides pretend the line isn't there, because if they didn't pretend, there would be ugly fighting everywhere.

The water tower is protected by a chain-link fence. A large sign shouts *Keep Out*. Through the rain, I can't see the top of the tank. I yank at the heavy padlock, but it doesn't give. I throw myself against the fence, but there are no weak spots. The only way in is to go up and over.

Barbed wire runs along the top, and I swing my feet wide to avoid it. But the sharp points prick my leg and arm. I feel cloth and skin ripping. I yelp and swear loudly. Chief better be up here.

The metal ladder is cold and slippery. I have to watch my grip as my hands are bloody from the barbed wire. I move quietly, afraid to startle anyone. The gangplank at the top is very narrow. Glancing between my feet down at the ground, I feel dizzy and hold the railing tightly. Just one quick look around and I'm getting out of here.

Chief is here, squatting on the gangplank, his back against the water tank. He stares over the town from under his baseball hat.

I approach slowly and sit by his side. The wind is strong up here. It drives the rain into my face. I need something to hold on to, something to keep me steady.

"How's it going?" I ask.

There's a long pause.

"How do you think?" he finally says.

"Your mom is phoning around, looking for you," I tell him. "She's really worried."

"Tell her this is not her fault." He bows his head and his words are muffled by his hoodie. "I chose to do this. All on my own."

"Your parents just lost Diane," I remind him. "What's it going to be like if you're not there?"

"They don't have to worry anymore." Finally he turns and looks at me. His face is wet from the rain. "All their lives they worry. And what good does it do?"

We hear the rumble of the train approaching, and then its shrill whistle. It roars under us and is gone.

"I'm going to China so that I can control my life," I say. My hands are trembling, so I tuck them into my armpits. "You're Canadian. You can control your life here."

"My people don't have hope in this country."

"Immigrants from around the world do."

"Not you."

Someone flicks a switch somewhere, and the streetlamps on Main Street, leading out to the freeway, go off. The night is over now.

"I'm going because I'm scared," I say. "You, you're not scared."

He doesn't answer, so I think I've made a point. "Can we go down?"

"Sure!"

He lunges forward and I scream. But he catches himself at the railing and then grins at me. "You sure are jumpy, China!"

Again I think I've won, so I stand. "Let's go."

He shakes his head. "It's the fast way down for me."

"If I stay," I plead, "I'll need your help to fight the drug charge."

"Get some lawyers."

"They'll be white."

He leans over the railing. "Go, China. Get the hell out of here."

I reach for him but he jerks away. I'm glad it's raining. If I'm crying, then he can't see it.

"Don't do this, please."

"Leave me alone," he hisses.

I shake so badly that I drop to my hands and knees. "Come down," I scream.

"Get away," he says.

I grab the railing and stand up. "If you go, I'll go too, right behind you."

He looks at me and snorts. "No you won't. You've got China."

"I'm not going," I tell him. "I changed my mind."

"Liar!"

"You said this was the best country in the world."

"I lied," he says quietly.

"I'll follow you," I declare, "right over that railing."

"Liar!" he says again.

"If you jump," I say, "then you won't know, will you?"

Chief stares at me with glittering eyes. I stare back.

Finally he says, "Okay, let's do this together."

"Together sounds good." I stand beside him. I lean forward over the railing just like him. "Say when."

I wait. I shut my eyes. I wait. And wait. But Chief never says a word.

I open my eyes. The rain has stopped and the sky is brighter. At the horizon, the clouds are white, not gray.

Chief is gone from the railing. He sits against the water tank. The morning light brings a glow to his face.

"Get away from the railing, China," he says. "You don't want to do anything stupid."

Paul Yee is a best-selling author of a number of titles including picture-books and the short story collection, *What I Did Last Summer*. Paul lives in Toronto, Ontario, and continues to be one of the foremost chroniclers of the Chinese-Canadian experience.